POETRY

CW01507349

*LITERARY TRANSLATION*
*& POETRY*

*LITERARY TRANSLATION*
*& POETRY*

*UEA MA*
*Creative Writing Anthologies*
*2023*

This diverse anthology comprises the latest work from the 2023 cohort of translators studying UEA's renowned Literary Translation MA.

*DANIEL HAHN*
# Foreword

*Making the Hard Choices*

Translation is all about making choices.
From the big-picture policy decisions (*Do I keep the rhymes? How should I recreate all the slang?*), to the micro stuff (*OK, I'm gonna put the comma in, no, take the comma out, no put the comma in, no take etc. ad infinitum*), every finished text, however inevitable it might seem to us readers, could have turned out differently in a thousand ways. Not every choice is conscious and deliberately weighed-out, of course, but they've happened all the same.

Before the textual wrangles, though, translators must make a foundational choice whether to embark on a particular text at all, or opt for some other. Of the six translators in this anthology, not one chose the easy option. The challenges in every text are immediately apparent; but they've been met, and with great assurance.

The landscape in which Anglophone translators work has changed considerably in the last couple of decades, and it's unquestionably more open and welcoming than it was. More is being translated, that work is more various, we have more readers and better conditions. There are more opportunities, and the way they're being distributed is fairer than it used to be. The scene is far from perfectly equitable or meritocratic (and for now we're still stuck with capitalism, which skews certain decisions in unpleasant directions), but it's *better*. Which is just as well – we need pluralism being valued in our culture urgently.

It's a good time to be starting out, then. I should add, though, in the interests of honesty, that some areas do remain more resistant to our attentions than others. Children's books and drama, both of which are particularly dear to my heart, are still slower off the mark – in the UK, at least. Our adult book publishers have widened their interests in recent decades, but our children's publishers and theatres remain frustratingly hard to persuade. But look at Olivia Prowse's translation of Maeterlinck, and you can imagine how our stages might be enriched with things like this so different from the Anglophone canon. Oh, and you'll see how hard translating it can be, too – this particular text especially, with those myriad pulls in different directions, forcing a translator to finding space for these staccato voices, neither everyday contemporary chat nor something quite stylised. Again, you'll find these pages full of good, confident choices, large and small.

Personally, I'm a cowardly sort of translator who avoids translating poetry whenever possible, and looking at Elena Goldenbow's and Clara Ehlers's work only confirms my suspicion that it would be beyond me. The Hesse poem comes to a translator with some evident formal expectations, which Goldenbow has chosen not to shy away from, choosing sometimes to privilege these formalities – the translation is never rigid but it does sit beautifully within its form; the Poschmann poems may look looser, but that's deceptive. Her poems are no less terrifyingly demanding – it takes nerve even to try these sorts of work, and real, sensitive linguistic flair and ingenuity to pull it off as these two new poets have done.

Now, some of the choices we translators make are of course really tiny, and if we're honest, well, how much can they actually matter? Do I go for a semi-colon or a comma? Word A or its synonym B? Trivial choices, certainly. But they add up. Style and voice are just an aggregating of all these minuscule decisions. Any translator of poetry could tell you that, obviously, but artful prose requires the same attention. Look at the consistency of tone achieved in Sarah Cowie's piece, how purposeful its voice. The story leads you somewhere quite startling, and you can't help but follow.

Or look at the sentences we find in the Arelis Uribe extract – the pace is controlled by sentence lengths, and some of them are really big – but also incredibly well-formed, never sprawling. These are choices, again: translator Issy Emmitt could have ignored the integrity of the author's sentence shapes, simplified at the expense of the pace, and frankly saved herself a lot of trouble; but instead she inhabits every part of the text, boldly creating supple new sentences, with a new integrity of their own.

Many and various are the ways in which texts can cause a translator trouble, and Shimanto Reza's choice of material is one of those pieces that could have gone wrong so very easily. But it never does. From the first lines, a reader gets that thrilling feeling, utterly unmistakeable, of a translator and a writer who are seriously committing to this work. Whoah, so we're really doing this thing! Not for the first time in this collection, there were moments when I thought, wow, I wish I could do that.

(Though I keep remembering that these translators are all just starting out and I've been translating for about a million years, so that's a bit annoying, actually.)

I've always believed that literary translators are naturally quite attracted to difficulty. And that's just as well. Starting-out translators are always told what a challenge it is to get into this profession, and it's true. (There is a great oversupply of translators and not nearly enough demand; sure, some languages do have slightly less over-supply than others, but they're often not the ones with any institutional funding behind them.) I don't think it's hard to make the case, in the abstract, that we ought to have more translation – and more exciting and more diverse translation – injected into our literary market; but that same market doesn't make it easy. Why on earth would someone choose this path? And besides all the financial and career-making challenges, the job of actually producing a really great translation is hard! That's the thing about literary translation: it is, simply, difficult to be good at it.

Well, these six translators are. And that's about as promising a start as one could hope for. I'm so glad to have been introduced to their work, and can't wait to read more from them all.


Daniel Hahn

*CECILIA ROSSI*
# Introduction

In Their Own Words
*Introducing Sarah, Clara, Issy, Olivia, Elena and Shimanto*

The translation project is an opportunity
to reflect on the ways in which I work,
the physical experience of translating: I have
noted the thoughts, words, impressions and images
that came to me in my encounter with the text. I am
leaving a mark on the text.

I want to visualise my process
in a call and response format
each translation articulating not an answer
but a question
                    to find one that is mine.
                    Translation
as queering the text –
write again to how we des
IRE SUCH FLESHES shifting space
        remember

my Self and the character's Self were already intimately entwined.
It was the 'right' choice
to keep the sentences in their original, lengthy state,
but I did not want them to feel forced –
they should be as natural an extension of my Self
as they are of the narrator. And I will carry
the results of this experiment
with me for a long time.
There is more I might want to be able to say,
to explain, to provide to the reader: [to invite them] to trust me,

to engage with my work, my translation,
to do so actively and curiously: [and to warn them]
to not do so blindly,
to be critical, to challenge,
to do so defiantly.

It really ended up taking me on a journey,
from a place where I thought I knew how to translate the text
and what different methods I was going to use
for different drafts,
to one where I was focusing on elements
that hadn't even crossed my mind at the outset.

And yet. There always seems to be something.
Something like a remainder,
something that doesn't fit,
that pulls us back into the text.
Should I leave a footnote to contextualize? Like Vladimir Nabokov –
copious footnotes
footnotes reaching up like skyscrapers.
Or go back, like my writer, who kept editing his story after publication.
Why shouldn't I do the same?


Cecilia Rossi
August 2023

Sarah Cowie is a literary translator working mainly from French to English. She completed her BA in French and Spanish at the University of Glasgow before starting her translation career. She enjoys translating contemporary prose fiction, with a focus on short stories and Francophone literature outside of France.

sarah-cowie@outlook.com

*The Time I Lost the North*

A translated short story by Mireille Gagné

In my life, I don't sleep. I've tried everything: bamboo pillows, silk pillows, orthopaedic beds, hypoallergenic sheets; taking the radio alarm away, putting it back; turning the clock back a few minutes, turning it forward, not looking at it; earplugs, relaxing music, yoga, sex; over-the-counter medicines, melatonin, homeopathic drops; and prescription medication for wiping out all traces of thought.

I've also tried to understand the reason or reasons why I can't sleep. I've seen a psychologist, an acupuncturist, a hypnotherapist, even a Mexican shaman who tried to ease my pain by rubbing eggs all over my body. I've searched through every drawer of my childhood, dissected and analysed every one of my failures. I've come to the conclusion that there is no conclusion, this is just me, like someone blind from birth: a chronic insomniac.

When the sun sinks below the horizon, a nameless dread climbs up my legs, up my spine, and quietly lodges itself in my chest. Time, minutes, hours blend into one another, speed up, slow down. I can no longer tell the difference between the tick tock of the clock and the beating of my own heart.

Last night was no different. I tossed and turned. This morning, half-asleep in bed, I listen to the weather forecast on the radio. Today, rain, wind, and hail in some areas.

*Please bring your umbrella when you drive your mother to the airport. The end of the world is scheduled for six pm.*

I wake with a start. I must have dozed off for a fraction of a second. Mechanically, I turn off my alarm and attempt getting up. The haze takes a good ten minutes to clear. As my thoughts start to wander, an image thrusts itself suddenly into my head. My mother!

I'd forgotten about her. I hurry out of bed and quickly get dressed. No time to eat. I'll get a sandwich at the airport. The moment I open the door, my phone rings. It's probably her getting impatient. I don't answer. I go downstairs, start the car, turn on the radio. A scientist seems to be describing an imminent catastrophic event. Warning signs... Unusual and historically unprecedented... The magnetic north pole has shifted to Siberia... Snow geese have not migrated...

The radio fades away in my head. I drive in a half-dream, like a sleep-walker. I focus on the road ahead, my eyes sting. Everything blurs in front of me. I count the telephone poles to keep me awake, to hold on to the wires, but I feel so exhausted.

Quietly, the apocalyptic announcements march on. Potential inversion of the poles... Unknown consequences... Phenomenon which could affect other migrating animals... Possibly humans... Catastrophe... Humanity at risk...

*Henri, your end is nigh!*

I shake my head and instantly snap out of my daydream. I really need to sleep tonight. I turn right and arrive at my mother's house. She's stood on the pavement, of course she is, stiff with impatience. I park the car and put her bags in the boot. Just try to ignore her ranting.

When we're sat down, I start the engine and turn on the GPS. A robotic voice asks me my destination. I obey and I wait. The thing starts repeating on a loop: 'Recalculating. Recalculating. Recalculating.' I tap the machine, repeat the name of the airport, in vain. 'No signal' flashes on the screen. I drop the steering wheel, frustrated. As I'm trying to figure out if I can get there without the GPS, I hear my mother sigh loudly.

I turn to look at her. All I can see is a black hole, anger, then dis-appointment, an old disappointment rooted deep in her chest, an emptiness, a void that's impossible to fill: I've never managed it.

My mother gets out and slams the door, calls a taxi and leaves without saying goodbye.

I remain there motionless for a few minutes, thinking about what just happened. She's probably right. It's true, I've never achieved anything significant in my life. I don't seem to make the right decisions, I'm never looking the right way, but I sleep so little. I've never had a stable job, never had a real girlfriend. OK, I've been out with a few interesting women. But after a few weeks of dating, I've always found a good excuse to end things: car accident, laid off at work, incompatible in bed, run out of mobile data, smiles too much, wants kids, doesn't want kids, bad haircut, gluten intolerant.

I turn off the GPS, irritated it isn't working. I took today off work to deal with my mother. Now I've got an entire day to kill before sunset. All these hours. The wait before it gets dark is what really eats away at me. My brain plays on a loop. I lose control of my thoughts, they turn disturbing, oppressive, thick. At least if I could distract myself with something... I have no interest in or excitement for anyone or anything.

I look out the window, the wind pushes the clouds over my head. I feel the need to get out of the city and mix my smell with the earth's.

How to get out of here? It's been so long that I no longer trust my sense of direction. I remember a girl I went out with, last year maybe. Mélanie... Yeah, that was it. She lived right next to the Félix-Leclerc bridge. She wasn't pretty exactly, but she was kind to me. I think she comforted me. Why did I leave her, actually? Was it her voice? Was she a bit overweight? I remember she helped me sleep.

Instinctively, I set off. The route comes back to me calmly. I recognise a corner shop, a bar, a block of flats. I've been driving for more than twenty minutes when I realise there is no one on the road. It looks like people are in hiding. Maybe they really believe this is the end of the world? Do I? I don't know... What would it really change for me, anyway? Isn't this what I've been waiting for all these years?

I arrive outside Mélanie's flat. There's movement inside. I find myself wondering what she's doing right now, if she's alone. I'd quite like to talk to someone.

Finally, I see the bridge. I cross it and come out on to a motorway surrounded by fields, barren at this time of the year. There's hardly any snow left on the ground. Still no one in sight. It's very windy. My car keeps veering, but I manage to stay on the road for a few hours before I take an exit. I turn right towards the river. I go down a hill. The feeling of being a cloud gliding through the sky. I drive for a few more minutes before I stop. Outside, not a sound, the silence shouts at the top of its lungs. The same void I feel at night that stops me sleeping. I take a deep breath. I start walking.

Right in the middle of a field, a tree stands straight, the only break in the landscape. It must have been left here to attract lightning. I walk towards it. A branch is broken. It looks strangely like a door. I go in, ducking my head. I stretch out on the ground and close my eyes. My thoughts stop. I fall into a deep sleep.

—

The sun is already well below the horizon when I wake up. It must be nearly six. I get up, numb with cold, and jump on the spot a few times to warm myself up. I blow on my hands.

It's then I hear cries, echoing. Not human cries; the cries of birds, coming from far away. I look up and the sight takes my breath away. Thousands of snow geese split the sky in two with the beating of wings and rage, geese who are finally returning home after waiting for a long, long time. I watch as they make their way north.

—

There is a thud behind me. I turn around. A snow goose is lying on the ground, its eyes wide open. It looks dead. I walk up to it. Its wing is bleeding. I lean forward to take a closer look and something hits me on the back of the neck. The weight of the world on my shoulders. I fall flat on my face, breathless, my body paralysed. A sharp pain takes up all the space in my chest. I feel my heart explode, pierced with a thousand lead shots. I can barely breathe. Suffocating. Out of the corner of my eye, I see another goose descending from the sky. This one is alive. It lands beside me and pokes its head into my back, as if tugging at a bulrush. I feel it lift me up and carry me with it. For a moment, I feel like I'm flying, heading north too. It's all clear in my mind, the way to go, it's all mapped out. I feel light.

—

When I open my eyes again, I'm still in the same spot. Two geese are lying next to me on the ground. I sit up calmly. My head feels like it's going to explode. In the sky, the geese fly on. I wait until they've all passed, vanished into the horizon.

Everything is clear now.

I get up and look north.

I know exactly where to go.

*CLARA EHLERS*

Clara Ehlers is a literary translator from German and Italian, specialising in poetry and LGBT* narratives.

clara_ehlers@t-online.de

© 2004, Grund zu Schafen, published in the Frankfurter Verlagsanstalt, Frankfurt am Main.
© 2002, Verschlossene Kammern, published in zu Klampen, Lüneburg.

**deer exercise**
over the highway drifting stripes
funnelled through forests, very strictly
measured white,
and we followed the jumps, the stretches
of this broken line, deer crossing,
slippery slope, at the rest areas lay
unconditionally sleeping banks, water-
welled wood and the brown curved
backs of the mountains of wounded fur-surfaces,
clear cutting, perished paths, and we,
at full speed, like wind simulations
between chest-high twigs,
antlers wrapped in cotton-wool jackets,
dull figment (fall-dreams)
five-pointer, finger-tip:
but
      we smelled of soap
      of violets and pond-water, in front of us
      the horrible completion of the coming
frost soon hard-hooved

**Glazes of January, carne vale**
and the thin deviations had bathed in
cold baths, in dips with ice-plugs,
sponges of Chemnitz White, brushes,
plastered shrubs, and
once hail fell, when we wandered over
railway sleepers, over the bit by bit
entirely buried hills, my voice floured,
mono-syllabication, I leant deeper into your scent
and swayed along next to you
like on eggs, like picture-perambulations
only on finger-tips, in the soapy light
we inhaled birch-trees, the soundless layers of air
right-turning left-turning crows,
breath in fancy dress between us and
this greed for touch A PLATEAU
WE TOOK ON A WALK, and something
towing along beside us and distanced itself,
later
the brightly sprinkled hills
already bowed lower

**wintry application with tea-lights**
a tenderness follows, a heart-beat, almost
order (flageolet):
a scattered frost, a piece of tin-foil, the
flashing eyes
'like these unsteady regions renounce themselves of us
bit by bit'
imitations and disguises, half stay
like on photo-copied snow (the secret
hide-outs: your single fogged-up
lens, I left soon-after,
for decency's sake) and let all touches
fall: quickly
leant on you
flickering places, a heart-beat
full of tea-lights, light bandages: I feel
the shoes, the snow-edges
a tenderness follows, a few refuge-points
gently moved aside, I have painted my fingertips
as if they were winter-proof

**sea-poem**
far out
swim
swinging, corpus only known in extracts
easy prey of the gaze and
gliding along on his own shadow

under the skin
we felt the unprotected points,
soft rosettes, turgid
like a bloated mirror-image on Christmas-baubles,

dusted, powdered, a
play-thing of the waves, of the sea-foam; their
sudden onset of winter,
the strong signs of wear on a far-off image

went, embalmed, on its way,
white cargo, a shrine to the
fleeting nature of feeling, he
set the water an internal standard

**mercy-asylum**
baroque urge to overflow,
the twitching lids, twitching legs,
thickly sugared sleep, sweet burden
this flesh and already out of your control,
already flowing in pictures, private
TV channel, rosy juice, that I swallowed,
you bolted your lips onto mine
and the body, pumping and dreaming
is remote-controlled

we're going on air, the limbs
touch, give signals, my
skin is filled with syrup, I stick
to you, late-night shows trickle away,
insubstantial feature-films, REM phases, zapping
the night edits us

I have an urge to overreact,
in your sleep you test
your hands' capacity,
test exotic fruit, stir
in hot compotes of swelling peaches,
plums, apricots, the pictures connect,
viscously I see the heart-chambers, slides
of fully sugar-coated walls,
a glimpse of light, a cooking studio that stabilises itself,
you pat me down until I get heavy,
transparent, shiny, the whole body candied

Issy Emmitt studied Spanish & Politics at the University of Bath before deciding that anyone contemplating going into UK Government had to have several screws loose, and pursued translation instead. She translates mostly from Spanish, sometimes from Portuguese, and occasionally from Catalan, and enjoys working with emotionally and stylistically complex prose from women and queer authors.

issyetranslates@gmail.com
issytranslates.co.uk

*Italia*

An abridged translation of Arelis Uribe's 'Italia'
from the 2016 short story collection *Quiltras*

Italia was always reading a book. Sometimes we'd lie down in the grass and I'd rest my head on her legs and her hair would tickle my face and she'd read me works by Pedro Lemebel, or *The Night Face Up*, reciting 'the wondrous dream had been the other' in her calm, raspy voice, while I gazed up at her mouth, at her straight, white teeth. Italia wrote hundred-word stories for the *Santiago en Cien Palabras* competition and went to workshops at Balmaceda 1215 and sometimes I'd go looking for her after class so we could get ice cream in Parque Forestal. Italia was called Italia because, having been exiled, her mother married an Italian, and when they came back, together, to Chile and had a daughter, they baptised her so in celebration of their return, and to ensure they would never forget what it was to live in exile. Italia was sixteen and studied at a private school where she was allowed to wear her own clothes and cycle in every morning. Italia said *nonos* instead of grandparents, and spoke various languages besides Spanish and had been to Europe and knew that from the day she finished school her life was going to continue on some other continent, far from here and far from me.

The first time I saw her was at a Pilates class at the municipal gym in Providencia. She had a blunt fringe and a long mane of hair that curled at the ends. I watched her in the mirror the whole hour. I liked her flushed cheeks, her dark eyebrows, and the inward curve of her slim legs. I imagined that my hand would fit there perfectly. I spoke to her at the end of the class, and we left together on our bikes. I lived in the city centre, on the twentieth floor of one of those new buildings near the Metro Universidad de Chile, and she lived in a suburban cul-de-sac, like the one in *Home Alone*, at the edge of San Cristóbal Hill. That first time we talked, we pedalled around the hill, and I dropped her at her front door. Her house intimidated me: the chimney, the dense thicket of trees, the huge station wagon parked out front. But a few weeks later, we were already exchanging long messages on our mobile phones, and she was lending me books, and I was rolling my fingers in the tips of her chestnut hair.

Italia would write me letters where she joined up words that I never imagined would make sense together. She would call me on the landline first thing in the morning and, instead of speaking, play La Noyée – the song from *Amélie* – and I would dream that the accordion was saying *come* or *don't go* or *me too*. I liked that she was called Italia and how she'd tell me about seeing the Mona Lisa in France, about how small it is, and how in England it rains so much that you can't leave the house. I asked her what it was like to travel by plane, and what the clouds looked like from above. I liked her pale skin and comparing her light brown freckles against my dark ones. I liked touching her skin, feeling enveloped by it, lost in the sort of complexion I had longed for as a teenager because at school all of us with black hair had been infatuated with the only blond boy in our year, who himself was infatuated with the only blonde girl, in a logic that wasn't so much racist as in keeping with the rules of the market; with the law of an excess of dark-skinned girls and a scarcity of blondes.

Sometimes after class, we'd just walk around with our bikes. We'd get to the hill and drop them to one side in amongst the trees, and touch each other over our clothes until nine, ten, eleven at night, when the riverbank was a cold breath, and flocks of runners would pass by, burning calories in their fluorescent windbreakers.

At the start, everything Italia told me made me happy, euphoric. Listening to her always made me hungry to learn more about her life. I wanted to know which books she had read, if she had done ballet or horse-riding, how old she was when she got braces, when she had learnt to swim. I imagined myself as the main character of her stories; it was me who had had her crooked teeth corrected aged eight, me who had gone to restaurants as a child and enjoyed meals far more sophisticated than just barbecue chicken and chips. It was me who had played with uncles who were film directors and university professors instead of ice-cream vendors and taxi drivers, and it was me who had spent every Saturday in January swimming in the pool on the garden terrace.

One afternoon we met in front of the gym and decided to skip class. We went to Parque Bustamante and bought a meat-free pizza from the stall next to the public library. We took it to go and ate it whilst we dipped our feet in the artificial lake. I said that the pizza was delicious, and Italia laughed and explained that it wasn't pronounced *pitsa* or *pisa* but *pizzzzza*, like a panicked mosquito. When Italia corrected me, it filled me with a strange bitterness. I liked that she pointed out my mistakes – I felt like it made me better, more worthy of being with her. But at the same time, it hurt to have not been born with all those little wisdoms that were supposedly necessary for a person to walk tall in the world.

That night, Italia invited me to her house for the first time. We rode uphill towards Pedro de Valdivia. I felt like I was floating instead of pedalling; the lights of passing cars merged with the park lamps and beamed inside my glasses like an orangey-green aurora borealis (Italia had explained to me what that was). We entered the house through the kitchen, and her Nana Carmen came out to greet us. She murmured *mi niña*, followed by the usual refrain of a concerned grandmother, and offered Italia a glass of warm milk which she turned down. Nana Carmen spoke to me fondly and, on seeing that Italia didn't want anything, stowed herself away in the room adjoined to the kitchen, like a rabbit in its burrow.

We walked hand in hand up a wooden staircase to the second floor. Italia in front and me behind. Although it was dark, I focused on her slim legs, on the inward curve where I knew my hand would fit. The bedroom we went into was big, big enough that it could hold my entire flat inside. It had a double bed and that surprised me too, because in my world double beds were for married couples, for parents; the children's beds were always singles, or bunkbeds to be shared and fought over with younger siblings.

Italia dropped to the floor, forgetting about turning on the lights. I settled down beside her and kissed her, and her mouth tasted like fresh water, like glossy magazine paper. I touched the inward curve of her legs and was flooded with a sudden tingling sensation. I touched her breasts underneath her t-shirt, and they were soft and they were small and I pictured them, rosy pink atop pale white skin. We wrapped our legs around each other and I squeezed against her, and she squeezed against me. I imagined her cheeks were flushed, like in our Pilates class, and I brushed her neck with my nose and stayed there, my head resting on her shoulder, moaning, panting, listening to her muffled cries. I took off my gym clothes and she hers and I dipped my tongue inside her navel and then returned to her mouth and she licked my left breast like a hungry infant and then I couldn't take any more and in seconds I was gone, crashed out on top of her.

We lay on the floor for a while, our skin sticky. After, we moved to her bed and fell asleep there. The thing I remember most from that night is the sheets. They were the softest, whitest sheets I had ever slept on in my life.

The next morning, her father woke us up early, knocking on the door and telling us to come downstairs for breakfast. On the table (all at the same time) there was jugo de frutilla (fresh), cheese (various types), and granola (I think). Her parents were natural conversationalists, like her.

They talked about their work. He was some sort of engineer, and she was a scriptwriter and university professor. They discussed the news as it played out on Radio Cooperativa and they asked me what I did, and how I had met Italia. I told them about our Pilates classes and about myself, how I had recently finished my teacher training, how I was working in a little school in Recoleta and how I had recently moved into the centre, into a flat I hoped to buy one day. They didn't ask me what my family did, or where I had lived before. Not for lack of interest, but out of tact. Or manners, as my father would've put it.

Around eleven, Italia's mother offered to take me to the city centre in her car. I was going to the Pontifica to give a talk to a group of gifted and talented students from schools all over Santiago, or something like that. I would've preferred to have gone by myself on my bike, but I couldn't refuse the offer: it was Italia and her mother versus me.

We walked down to the car, and Italia's father helped me load my bicycle. Italia wanted to come with us and settled into the front passenger seat. I got into the back, by myself. Italia put on a few CDs to introduce me to the French music she loved so much, singers and songs I had never heard of before. She and her mother chatted in the front and threw the odd question back to me, like children playing Hot Potato. My replies were short, insubstantial. I was absorbed by the view out of the window, enraptured by the heart of Providencia, by the intense greenery on the streets and the immense size of all the houses.

We turned onto Avenida Portugal and Italia's mother parked the car and offered me a ticket for the metro, asking if I had topped up my *Bip!* card, if I needed money to get home. I answered honestly that no, thank you very much, but I was planning on cycling back. Italia looked at me, her brows furrowed, and her mother bristled. I didn't understand. I fumbled with getting my bike out of the car and Italia said goodbye with a cold gesture, which unsettled me.

In the weeks that followed we saw each other at Pilates, but I didn't always cycle her home. The messages and evening phone calls got more and more infrequent. Italia distanced herself from me, and I from her, in a slow but continuous rhythm, like two pieces of land in continental drift. I no longer enjoyed picturing myself in her stories. It hurt, that it had only ever been an exercise in invention. I was terrified that the moment might come when I had to invite her to my house. I couldn't see myself bringing her to Quilicura on the minibus, introducing her to my mother, growing fatter every day; to my father, talking with his mouth full in front of the television; to a pallid, apathetic version of myself, sat in the tiny living room with its cheap vinyl flooring.

So I hid. I stopped going to Pilates. I changed my phone number. Until I didn't see her anymore. But I can guess exactly what became of her. I know that she finished school, that she flew through the university entrance exam and that she went to Europe anyway, with her *nonos*. I know that she ultimately ended up in Florence or Barcelona or a city like that, and that she studied photography or painting or marionette theatre. I know that she got together with some tall European, and lived with him in an apartment with an open, panoramic view of a beautiful, historic city.

Sometimes I'd pedal through Santiago and imagine bumping into her. I thought about how she might see me and think of me, how she might long for the afternoons that we spent lying in the grass and reading in one of the parks. I liked to fantasise about the possibility of being seen by her, and never knowing.

One night I cycled down Barrio Bellavista, past the shops where we used to steal books, thinking that it would be an apt place to run into her. And then she appeared. She had cut her hair short, like Twiggy. She walked out of the library with a group of people, smiling with her perfect teeth. We passed each other. It was quick, less than a second. I zoned in on her face and my chest tightened, delighted or terrified, I don't know. She looked back at me, that human instinct to react to a foreign gaze, to defend oneself from a possible predator. I thought I saw a spark of nostalgia on her face, though I'm not entirely sure. I didn't stop to check. I just pushed my feet harder, cycling faster and faster along the pavement.

OLIVIA M. PROWSE

Olivia M. Prowse is an Australian and British translator. She studied French and German at the University of Bristol and works from both languages into English. She specialises in theatre translation, and her interests include migrant literature, work from minoritised speaker communities, and trans and queer stories.

prowseom@gmail.com

*Pelleas and Melisande*

## A translated drama by Maurice Maeterlinck:
## Act IV, Scenes III & IV

*To Octave Mirbeau.*
*As a token of deep friendship, admiration, and gratitude.*
*M.M.*

CHARACTERS

ARKEL, King of Allemonde

GENEVIEVE, mother of Pelleas and Golaud

PELLEAS, Golaud, Arkel's grandsons

MELISANDE

YNIOLD, Golaud's young son (from a previous marriage)

A DOCTOR

THE PORTER

SERVANTS, poor people, etc.

ACT IV

SCENE III

*A castle terrace. Little Yniold is trying to lift a large stone.*

| | |
|---|---|
| Yniold: | Oh! this stone is heavy!... It is heavier than me... It is heavier than everyone in the world... It is heavier than everything that has happened. |
| | *(Beat.)* |
| Yniold: | I can see my golden ball between the rock and this awful stone, and I cannot reach it... My little arm is not long enough... and this rock does not want to be lifted... I cannot lift it... and nobody could lift it... It is heavier than the whole house... it seems as though it were rooted deep in the earth... |
| | *(From far off, the bleats of a flock of sheep.)* |
| Yniold: | — Oh! oh! I can hear the sheep crying. |
| | *(Yniold goes to the edge of the terrace to look.)* |
| Yniold: | Look! The sun is gone... The little sheep are coming; they |

are coming... There are so many!... There are so many!... They are scared of the dark... They are huddling together! They are huddling together!...

They can barely walk any more... They are crying! they are crying! and they are going so fast!... they are going so fast!... They are already at the big crossroads.

Ah! Ah! They do not know which way to go now... They have stopped crying... They are waiting... Some would like to go right... They would all like to go right... They cannot!... The shepherd threw some dirt at them...

Ah! Ah! They are going to come this way... They are obeying! They are obeying! They are going to go under the terrace... They are going to go under the rocks... I am going to see them up close...

Oh! Oh! There are so many of them! There are so many!... The whole road is covered with them...

Now they are all quiet... Shepherd! Shepherd! Why have they stopped speaking?

Shepherd *(out of sight)*: Because this is not the way to the barn, now...

Yniold: Where are they going? — Shepherd! shepherd! — Where are they going? — He cannot hear me now. They are already too far away... They are going fast... They are not making noise any more... That is not the way to the barn, now... Where are they going to sleep tonight? — Oh! Oh! — It is too dark... I am going to say something to someone...

*(Yniold exits.)*

SCENE IV

*A fountain in the park. Enter Pelleas.*

Pelleas:    This is the last night... the last night... Everything has to
            stop... I have played like a child around something I never
            suspected... I have played in a dream around the snares of
            destiny... What woke me so suddenly? I am going to run
            away, crying in joy and pain like a blind man fleeing his
            burning house... I am going to tell her that I am going to
            run away... My father is out of danger; and I cannot lie to
            myself any longer... It is late; she is not coming... I would
            do better to leave without seeing her again... I have to get
            a good look at her this time... There are things I cannot
            remember now... Sometimes it feels like it has been a
            hundred years since I saw her... And I still have not held
            her gaze in mine... There is nothing left for me if I leave
            like this. And all these memories... it is as if I were carrying
            a drop of water in a muslin bag... I have to see her one
            last time, to the bottom of her heart... I have to tell her
            everything I have not said...
            *(Enter Melisande.)*
Melisande: Pelleas!
Pelleas:    Melisande! — Is it you, Melisande?
Melisande: Yes.
Pelleas:    Come here; do not stay at the edge, in the moonlight. —
            Come here. We have so many things to say to each other...
            Come here into the shadow of the linden tree.
Melisande: Let me stay where it is bright...
Pelleas:    Someone might see us from the tower windows. Come
            here; here, we have nothing to be afraid of, — Take care;
            someone could see us...
Melisande: I want them to see me...
Pelleas:    What is the matter? Were you able to get out without
            being seen?
Melisande: Yes; your brother was asleep...
Pelleas:    It is late. — In an hour they will close the gates. We must be
            careful. Why did you come so late?
Melisande: Your brother was having a bad dream. And then my robe

caught on the nails of the door. See, it is torn. I lost all that
time, and I ran...

Pelleas: My poor Melisande!... I would be almost afraid to touch you (*beat.*) You are still out of breath, like a hunted bird... Is it for me, for me that you do all this?... I can hear your heart beating as if it were my own... Come here... closer, closer to me...

Melisande: Why are you laughing?

Pelleas: I am not laughing; — or else I am laughing out of joy, without knowing it... Perhaps it would make more sense to cry...

Melisande: We have come here again... I remember...

Pelleas: Yes... yes... Long months ago. — So, I did not know... Do you know why I asked you to come tonight?

Melisande: No.

Pelleas: It is maybe the last time I will see you... I have to go away for ever...

Melisande: Why do you say you are going away for ever?

Pelleas: Must I tell you what you already know? — You do not know what I am going to tell you?

Melisande: No, no; I know nothing...

Pelleas: You do not know why I have to distance myself... you do not know that it is because... (*he suddenly kisses her.*) I love you...

Melisande (*in a hushed voice*): I love you too (*beat.*)

Pelleas: Oh! Oh! What did you say, Melisande!... I almost did not hear it!... We have broken the ice with red-hot irons!... You said that with a voice that came from the end of the world!... I almost did not hear you... You love me? — You love me too?... When did you first love me?

Melisande: I always did... Ever since I first saw you...

Pelleas: Oh! The way you said that!... It was like your voice was gliding over the ocean in springtime!... I had never heard it until now (*beat.*) it feels like rain has fallen on my heart!... You said it so clearly!... Like I had asked an angel!... I cannot believe it, Melisande!...

Why would you love me? — But why do you love me? — Is what you said true? — You are not trying to deceive me? — You are not lying to me a little, to make me smile?

Melisande: No, I would never lie; I only lie to your brother...

Pelleas: Oh! The way you said that!... Your voice! your voice... It is fresher and clearer than water... It is like pure water on my lips! (*beat*.) It is like pure water on my hands...

Give me, give me your hands... Oh! your hands are small!... I did not know you were so beautiful!... I have never seen something so beautiful, before you...

I was restless, I searched everywhere in the house... I searched everywhere in the countryside... And I never found beauty... And now I have found you! I have found you!... I do not believe there is a more beautiful woman on earth!... Where are you? — I cannot hear your breathing now...

Melisande: It is because I am looking at you...

Pelleas: Why are you looking at me so gravely? — We are already in shadow. — It is too dark under this tree. Come into the light. We cannot see how happy we are. Come, come; we have so little time left...

Melisande: No, no; let us stay here... I am closer to you in the darkness...

Pelleas: Where are your eyes? — You are not going to run away from me? — You are not thinking of me now.

Melisande: But I am, I am; I am thinking only of you...

Pelleas: You were looking somewhere else...

Melisande:  I saw you somewhere else...

Pelleas: You are distracted... What is the matter? — You do not look happy to me...

Melisande: But I am, I am; I am happy, but I am sad...

Pelleas: We are often sad, when we love each other...

Melisande: I always cry when I think of you...

Pelleas: Me too... me too, Melisande... I am always near you; I cry for joy and yet...

(*Pelleas kisses Melisande again.*)

Pelleas: — You are strange when I kiss you like that... You are so beautiful that it seems like you are about to die...

Melisande: You too...

Pelleas: There it is, there it is... We do not do what we want... I did not love you the first time I saw you...

Melisande: Me neither... me neither... I was afraid...

Pelleas:      I could not meet your eyes... I wanted to leave straight
              away... and yet...
Melisande:  I did not want to come, myself... I still do not know why
              I was afraid of coming...
Pelleas:      There are so many things we will never know... We are
              always waiting; and then...    What is that noise? — They
              are closing the gates!...
Melisande:  Yes, they have closed the gates...
Pelleas:      We cannot get back in! — Do you hear the bolts? — Listen!
              listen!... the big chains!... the big chains!... It is too late, it is
              too late!...
Melisande:  Good! good! good!...
Pelleas:      You?... There it is, there it is!... It is no longer us who want
              it!... Everything is lost, everything is saved! Everything is
              saved tonight! — Come! Come... My heart is beating madly,
              right up to my throat...
                  *(Pelleas embraces Melisande.)*
Pelleas:      Listen! Listen! my heart is on the verge of strangling me...
              Come! Come!... Ah! it is so fine in the shadows!...
Melisande:  There is someone behind us!...
Pelleas:      I do not see anyone...
Melisande:  I heard a noise...
Pelleas:      All I can hear is your heart in the darkness...
Melisande:  I heard the crack of dead leaves...
Pelleas:      The wind has gone quiet all of a sudden... It died down
              while we were kissing...
Melisande:  Our shadows are so big tonight!
Pelleas:      They embrace right down to the depths of the garden...
              Oh! they kiss so far from us!... Look! Look!...
Melisande (*breathlessly*): A-a-h! — He is behind a tree!
Pelleas:      Who?
Melisande:  Golaud!
Pelleas:      Golaud? — where? — I do not see anything...
Melisande:  There... in the depths of our shadows...
Pelleas:      Yes, yes; I saw him... Let us not suddenly turn around...
Melisande:  He has his sword...
Pelleas:      I do not have mine...
Melisande:  He saw us kiss...
Pelleas:      He does not know that we have seen him... Do not move;

do not turn your head... He would strike. . . (B*eat.*) He will stay there as long as he thinks we do not know... He is watching us...

He is still not moving... Get out of here, get of here right now... I will wait for him... I will stop him...

Melisande: No, no, no!...

Pelleas: Go! Go! He saw everything!... He will kill us!...

Melisande: Good then! Good! Good!...

Pelleas: He is coming! He is coming!... Your lips!... Your lips!...

Melisande: Yes!... Yes!... Yes!...

(*They kiss frantically.*)

Pelleas: Oh! Oh! All the stars are falling!...

Melisande: On me, too! On me, too!...

Pelleas: Again! Again!... Give! Give!...

Melisande: Everything! Everything! Everything!...

(*From the shadows, Golaud rushes at them, sword in hand, and strikes Pelleas, who falls at the edge of the fountain. Melisande flees, terrified.*)

Melisande (*fleeing*): Oh! Oh! I have no courage!... I have no courage!...

(*Golaud pursues Melisande through the wood, in silence.*)

*ELENA GOLDENBOW*

Elena Goldenbow was born in Germany and has lived in the UK on and off since 2013. She studied American Literature and Creative Writing at the University of East Anglia. As a translator she mostly focuses on prose, but wanted to challenge herself for this anthology and translate a poem her mother introduced her to at fourteen when she first moved to the UK.

elena.stroeher@googlemail.com

"Stufen" from: Hermann Hesse, Sämtliche Werke in 20 Bänden. Edited by Volker Michels. Band 10: Die Gedichte. © Suhrkamp Verlag Frankfurt am Main 2002. All rights belonging to and reserved by Suhrkamp Verlag Berlin.

*Stages*

A translation of a poem by Hermann Hesse

As every flower must fade and every youth
Gives way to years, so blossoms each life stage.
So flowers every wisdom, every truth
Within its time and cannot stay ongoing.
When called by life, the heart must be assuaged,
Ready for a new beginning and farewell.
Giving itself with courage, without mourning,
To other bonds that every day arrive.
And each beginning holds a certain spell
To shield us and to help us stay alive.

Cheerfully, room to room we must go striding,
Not to seek in any one a final home.
The world spirit wants not to chain or narrow
It wants to lift us; stage by stage, and widen.
Just when we've made a home in our surroundings
So comfortably lived in, we grow fatigued.
Just those prepared for leaving, journeying
May shirk the crippling force that habit wields.

Perhaps even on the day death is descending
It carries us, young again, to someplace other.
The call of life to us is never ending...
Well then, my heart, bid farewell and recover!

Shimanto Reza is a translator from Dutch and Italian. He grew up bilingual (English and Dutch) in Belgium, lived for three years in Italy, and also works as a freelance editor. His Dutch essays and stories have been published in journals such as *DW B, De Revisor* and *Hard//hoofd*.

reza.shimanto@gmail.com

*An Incomplete Catalogue of Ruins and Utopias*

A translated short story by Dutch writer Christiaan Ronda, originally published in *Kluger Hans #42 Chaos*

*I. The villa in the winter quarters of the State Circus of the GDR in Hoppegarten, Brandenburg*

says, The opposite of order is a ruin – faded glory, entropy petrified, try tryer tryest fail and the villa says, A ruin is a building who's mislaid her Sunday best, sat there in a damp kitchen sat there in some old bathrobe and with unbrushed teeth, no: in her unbrushed grey hair a wig of wolves' locks, the teeth (like a bear trap like a wind-up toy) left on the night stand in a glass of evaporated water and the ruin straightens her bathrobe and sighs and explains, A ruin is a country that does exist and does not exist and she says, A ruin is a clown who after removing his makeup can't go home – it's all a show, a performance and she takes a long, long GDR drag of an Inka cigarette and she says, *Show*, *performance*, all these Anglicisms, as if we can't find our own words or invent them if need be, language a deboned ruin graffiti sprayed all over the adjectives, *paradigm shifts* and *bucket lists* crowd in and weigh on our already cracked-up concrete, gravity has pulled everything down and now time is slowly doing the rest and she takes another drag and says, It's sheer performerei, utter Afführungigkeit and deep deep sorrow, the paint is wiped off the kloun the kloun looks in the mirror and is fed up and the ruin licks her lips as if she can already taste the iron barrel and she laments: Words bricks trust fags permits mercy art – save us or drop us, care for me or let me die but don't keep us trapped in limbo this liminal no-place where you mustn't be or become, you mustn't moan or rot, no essence or existence, and she says, A ruin is a thought resisted by the future and feared by nostalgia and it's hard to make out the words the video's glitchy, old tape, and she says, Mankind's a ruin and civilization's a ruin and the desert's a ruin and the everlasting verdant jungle's a ruin, a ruin every statue and every plaque and every flag and every tombstone and every movie and every novel and she says, A ruin every fence and every gate and every nuclear plant and every refugee camp and *Es ist niemals ein Dokument der Kultur, ohne zugleich ein solches der Barbarei zu sein* and she says, Every ruin waits for a brief moment of inattention to collapse we've been going for so long but you keep restoring not-restoring permitting retracting dredging pushing under, just let me be anthill honeycomb let me disappear or give me some purpose this implosion can't go on forever can it? can it? and she says, A ruin is nothing but a monument to impotence, a misshapen memorial to an omission and she looks at something outside the frame and says, What were we talking about? and she sighs and she's quiet and she takes a drag and she

## II. The shield of a giant tortoise in the surf of San Salvador, Ecuador

Lately I find myself having to stand still and consider whether a thought I'm having is a memory or a dream. I wonder what this means: Is my imagination growing stronger or my memory growing weaker? *Standing still* here is of course a metaphor: my mind stays in place for a minute or two, then gets back on its way – for centuries my physical dimension has lain dead, empty and pointless on the beach. Flesh and nerves and eyeballs and muscle and sinew and bone gone: a shield is what I am, both pointless destruction and pure essence: without the shield the animal is unrecognisable after all. It's all the same, my mind strolls about the island all the same, will keep strolling until the seas or volcanoes swallow everything up and make the planet a ruin and all days are past and all will finally be quiet.

They consumed me, years and years ago. It's my own fault – tortoise meat is supposed to be one of the tastiest kinds of meat in the world. They came. Every ruin's story ends with a departure and it begins with an arrival: they came in boats, or: they came in tanks, or: they came in wagons, or: they came on foot. They came, ruins begin with intruders. Can you hear me, is the surf a bit loud? Not that I could mute it, but I can try and speak up.

They came in boats and I was curious and then I was no more. Or perhaps every ruin starts with a utopian desire: if we hadn't at some point believed in the future we wouldn't have built this world, but now that this future has turned out to be an impossibility we let the world decay. *Soñamos con utopía y nos despertamos gritando.* The shield of a giant tortoise in the surf of an island in the Pacific isn't a lot more ridiculous than an Egyptian pyramid in the desert or an Inca pyramid in the jungle or a Communist pyramid in the heart of Tirana. Yes, in everything, in all tries and shows and revolutions and works of masonry and coalition agreements and temple complexes and declarations of love and capitulations and started manuscripts – in everything the contours of a future pile of rubble can already be made out. The only thing that always survives violence and forgetfulness is the imagination. There is no art in heaven, so heaven is hell.

The best way to prepare a giant tortoise for consumption is exactly what you're now imagining it to be.

### III. A black-and-white photograph of a wooden model of a planned Soviet monument in Moscow, USSR

In the future we'll all talk straight, straight-arrowed and straight-aimed, or we won't talk at all; better not talk, but do – undertake – execute – underfeed – deny – defund and defenestrate all naysayers and angstgegners. Babel can be built if only we find the right screws. Lopsided Tatlin hills rise concentrically in utopian near misses … A monument is a mausoleum for the future, the hypothetical future which in the actual future will be hopelessly outdated, and what is a memorial that was never built?— simulacrum. Faceless obscurity awaits all – worn out – polished smooth – all edges sanded off by the wind. Anonymously we surf on marble boards through eternity and all that remains and all that will persist and all that will be left to see will be the ossified future machines, the monuments to moments, broken molars that stick stories-high out of the black sand in honour of that which can never exist: the future, the only thing that by the grace of itself can never step into reality. The future itself is a paradox
    paradox, paradox, parody
            *From things about to disappear, I turn away in time.*
            *To watch them out of sight, no, I cannot do it.*
                    and a thousand years pass, an amnesiac mercy.

### IV. A demented woman in a care home in Luddel, the Netherlands

On the wall there are posters of animals and prints of landscape paintings. The calendar of the local history society. Easy-to-digest, amusing, psychoinactive non-stimulants. Deadly, that is – death on the wall, death by a thousand bores, *Here, look at nothing.* Wouldn't it be far more stimulating to put up a Braque poster? A Remedios Varo? Or aren't we stirring up the Alzheimer's bourgeoisie anymore? The ship's sinking, it can't be helped, and the only job of the care home is to make the way to the bottom as comfortable as possible. I take a quick swig of whisky. A woman in a wheelchair sees me. I put the flask back in my inside pocket and she winks at me. I grin and wink back, but she's already looking at one of the nurses who's come in with a tray, and she winks again. A winking machine.

There are more old women here than old men. One of those women is suddenly standing next to me. Big glasses, sunken yellow face, big ears and a thin mouth, she's a wig-wearing Eichmann in his glass box in Jerusalem. Dementia is the banal evil: no cause, no secretive or sinister skulduggery, no ulterior motive. If only there was some intention, some hatred – then at least we'd have something to rage against. *Je suis un cimetière abhorré de la lune.* Without any future or past. The woman places a Grim Reaper hand on my forearm and gently tugs me along to a room down the hall, a small room with a single bed, heavy wooden furniture and all manner of frames and knickknacks. Then I understand what's going on and I shudder: the poor soul wants to show me her room. Without a word and with her hand fixed firmly on my arm she leads me around that hollow cube full of unintelligible memories, paraphernalia which can only amuse you if you know the story behind them, and she has no idea where that big seashell came from, the plaster mask, the copper incense burner, though she has kept an unshakeable sense of property, of pride in her possessions, *I haven't much left and what I have got has become inscrutable, but it is* mine, *that much I can say.* I nod, I smile, make soothing noises like she's a cat, and she squeezes my arm in gratitude or confusion. When we've gone around the room, she doesn't seem to know what to do, and I say, Shall we go for a walk? She shrugs like it's all the same to her, *Whatever* – yes, she has the look on her face of a bored teenager. I laugh and she grins and together we make our way back to the living room, where immediately I lose my new chum to a plastic bowl of pink pudding.


*V. A museum under construction*

religious junkies stuff their lidless eyes full of glass splinters and shout
    that they can see Jesus and Krishna and
four women naked from the waist up laugh maniacally as they chuck
    an unconscious man in the grey canal, he's speared by a rusty
    handlebar but doesn't awake and
on the seventieth floor of a block of flats where the lifts aren't working,

hunger-hollowed tenants rip wet innards from the still-warm
carcass of a rhinoceros who's lost its way and
two teens with tattoo-filled faces in the courtyard of an abandoned fire
station shyly explore each other's lips in the glow of a pyramidal
bonfire of diapers, computer keyboards and shrink-wrapped truffles
and

> *before I go, I think I should tell you*
> *that all the stars are dying and*
> *most of them are already through*
> *we're just getting off on yesterday's fire* and

deep in the belly of a rusty oil rig thirteen naked figures dance rousing
hoops to Ravel's *Boléro* until the day has passed and all days have
passed and
an ageless man in a peacock feather dress floats along the street, pulled
by a pack of poison-drooling Komodo dragons on long leashes and
a broken vagrant urinates on the gate of a former biscuit factory and loudly
declaims a forgotten poem by Rimbaud or Verlaine and
while the eye descends from the clouds onto the carpet of concrete and
neon and fluttering plastic, an earthquake on the horizon tears
through and before you can start begging for mercy five, six
skyscrapers have disappeared, the rupture propagates, brand-
new nuclear plants and distribution centres are swallowed whole,
overground trains turn into underground trains turn to iron powder,
Ferlinghetti screams a cackling dirge to the world, a whole shopping
street full of paper bags and modern people disappears in the blink
of an eye into cracks with some red glow far, far below and we settle
into the short-lived heat and, why not, flip another tortoise onto its
back to cook it over the lava until we're left with nothing but ruins.

*ACKNOWLEDGEMENTS*

It goes without saying that our thanks must go first and foremost to our wonderful course tutors – Cecilia Rossi, Tom Boll, and Duncan Large – who have guided our learning, imparted great wisdom, and entertained our boisterous (and frankly, often very *loud*) debates. Our classes have been the lifeblood of this programme, and we cherish the hours we have spent interacting with such generous teachers.

Furthermore, we must thank the incredible array of translators who have given up their time to workshop with us: Don Bartlett, Christina MacSweeney, Jen Calleja, Timberlake Wertenbaker, Jayasree Kalathil, Sophie Stevens, Mónica Maffía, Miriam Tobin, Gabriel Torem, and Jean Boase-Beier. These talks have provided us with the answers to every how, what, when, who and why we could possibly think up.

We would also like to thank the many other individuals and organisations who have helped foster such a productive and welcoming environment: Helen Busby at the Archive, the BCLT staff, the Sainsbury Centre exhibitions, and the UEA librarians who have acquired the many, many books that we would have otherwise spent our life savings on importing, post-Brexit.

Finally, perhaps the most important lesson we have learned this year is that translation is an inherently collaborative process; our work flourishes not only as a result of the relationships we form with our authors, but from the ideas, advice, and support we exchange with our fellow translators. So let us all raise our bookmarks to the 2023 MA Literary Translation cohort (and our lovely part-timers too). It is rare for a group of people from all walks of life to click so immediately, and rarer still for that initial connection to bloom into such strong, affable, and uproarious friendships. We have been lucky to an almost unfathomable degree.

Sarah Cowie, Clara Ehlers and Issy Emmitt.

This diverse collection showcases work from the 2023
cohort of poets studying UEA's renowned Poetry MA

*BHANU KAPIL*
# Foreword

*Where do poems come from? How do they arrive?*

I am thinking of two conversations, one with a poet and one with a person who loved to recite poetry, but did not write it. Perhaps the answers to these floating questions are held within those conversations, fifty years apart, and also in the poems of the anthology you are about to read.

Conversation 1: In the Iris Café, Mina Gorji said, "I think of the poem as storing something." We were talking, I think, about migration* and memory. How a poem stores something that's not recorded, let's say, in the document of place. Something small. Something fleeting. Something you will never touch or smell again. A glimpse. A juxtaposition of colours that does not recur in the present: navy-blue and burnt orange, for example. The kind of poem I'm trying to describe does not explain or place the sensations prompted or evoked by intense or high contrast. Neither (unlike the questions) do they float.

*I recall seeing Ana Mendieta's *silueta* series for the first time, in Des Moines, Iowa. How the "exogenous red" made me cross the gallery space to be in front of it. To make her *siluetas*, Mendieta lay down on the earth to form the physical outline of her body, then re-filled that outline with vermillion powder, earth, smoke, flowers, or the sea itself, a residual foam as the tide came in. She wrote, "I am overwhelmed by the feeling of having been cast from the womb (nature). My art is the way I re-establish the bonds that unite me to the universe. It is a return to the maternal source." Yes, I understood that, the desire for what you're making to be the means by which you, the practitioner, might adhere to planetary time. Or listen for it.

Consider Mina Gorji's "Ground Ash Ghazal," which you can read online in the *Poetry Birmingham Literary Journal*, in which she notes: "Blue smoke curling / from the crater, scent of flowers." Two senses are bundled here, but also two scales, as Gorji has put it elsewhere. I experience moments like this, in a poem, as a confluence. A place where two rivers meet. It's here that I am prepared to wait, for a long time, for what is as yet to emerge. To "Hear the rain, listening / for tomorrow's flowers." That's the last line of Gorji's poem, and it's here that I turn to the second conversation I'd like to place (or store) in this foreword, a long-ago memory of my grandfather's stories of his long journeys across a region now impassable with wild freedom.

Imagine a new bride waving goodbye to her husband, who mounts a white Arabian horse, a violin strapped to his back, a set of watercolors in a satchel, a chess-set and notebook tucked in. My grandfather rode on this horse from Lahore to Akshabad (in present day Turkmenistan) then back towards Peshawar, Jalalabad, Bhulan, his ancestral village, then onwards again. He'd return having memorized the poems of these places, living with tribal groups or in cities for months at a time, learning to write and speak new dialects or languages. As we lay on our jute cots beneath the stars, he'd recite those poems by heart. He'd transcribed them, of course. But one night, mid-century, it was time to go. To leave. Abruptly. As so many people did. Time to go. To burn the notebooks, the poems, everything that couldn't be carried, and to scrape that ash into a small container. Imagine a tiny box of ash. This is what my grandfather carried across a border that had formed overnight.

This is how a poem might be stored.

When I turn to the poems in this anthology, I'm curious about what they trace, keep, release or burn in turn. How they're arriving, imagining, traversing, remembering and reaching even now. Perhaps I'll close with a list, a way of storing my glimpses of these extraordinary, funny, and unruly poems, with gratitude to all the poets who have contributed to this beautiful anthology. Keep writing, poets. Don't stop.

Imagine: "ghee rhythmically beaten / with soft jelly tricep" (Lillian Akampurira Aujo).

Hear: "fireworks / without being able to see them" (Freya Bantiff).

Traverse: "this raw light new to me" (Alice Bridgwood).

Remember: "Billie reading, / stringing herself out to fit in the crook / of a book (Jessa Brown).

Love: "like a budget wine, / when she would swill him in her glass" (Isabelle Crow).

Write: "the shape of things to come" (Rupert Dorey).

Metabolise: "eyeroll wetly in skull" (E. M. Fawkes).

Picture: "a torch in her hand / this vegetable you have never eaten warm (Kana Hozoji).

Keep remembering: "what you don't say about the sun" (Tanuvi Joe).

Or: "break open the water like an egg" (Lauren Sheerman).

Undo: "each day's stains, the claim / to make us new (Harriet Truscott).

Reach: "river flowing backwards / viscus flowers blooming" (Adrienne Wilkinson).

Walk: "home with neighbours" (Rebecca Zeman).


Bhanu Kapil
Cambridge, June 2023

*SOPHIE ROBINSON*
## Introduction

Teaching is both a humbling and a transcendent experience. This is my ninth year teaching the MA in Poetry at UEA, and I have never failed to be surprised, enriched, educated and enlivened by working with a group of MA poets. This year was no exception. From 2pm to 5pm every Tuesday, through storms and snow and an endless winter, into the wobbly sunshine of springtime and the smell of fresh cut grass, groups of us sat in the round and listened, read, wrote, talked. After so many years of running workshops it can be easy for me to think I have 'got' the poem, that I have a handle on it, that there's some omniscient birds-eye view I've arisen to through sheer repetition of the workshop format. But what you can't count on, and what makes teaching a spiritual experience, is the aliveness of the workshop: a tangle of language, perspectives, emotions, ideas, cultures, nervous systems.

I learned something new from each poet I taught this year: a new word, a new historical fact, a new way to express a feeling, a new way to use a verb, a new way to create an image, a new way to work with form or verse, a new way to break a line in half or make an 'old' idea brand new. Poetry is an imprecise art, and so much rests on the subjectivity and body of the speaker and reader, and on the unpredictable relationship between the two of them, invented, in each poem, anew. Each workshop is an exercise in risk, spontaneity, vulnerability, collaboration and testing this connection. Work shared by students in draft form in these workshops is often its debut, its first time being heard and witnessed outside of the page and the writer's mind. It is a life-giving process, allowing these fresh poems to be made 'real' through a kind of communal devotion and focus of attention in the sacred space of the group.

This collection work is the result of these magical workshops, and the hard work of the poets between then and now. The breadth, depth, scope and ambition of the work here astounds me, and having the kind of job where I watch a group of talented writers take life-changing risks week after week, show up for each other, draft and redraft, be each others' first readers, and trust me to lead the process, is an honour that never gets old. I only hope you enjoy being a reader of these poems as much as I have enjoyed it, over and over and newer each time.

Sophie Robinson
June 2023

Lillian Akampurira Aujo is a Ugandan writer. Her work has been published by *HarperVia*, *Transition*, *Prairie Schooner*, and *Jalada Africa*. She is the recipient of a Global Voices Scholarship at UEA. Her poetry explores lineage, absentee fatherhood, and the marginal places women are forced to occupy in such patriarchal narratives.

lillianaujo80@gmail.com

## Markings

Your palm is a dark smoky canvas
the lines etched there are old soot
your eye-whites are rheum-ed with brown,
everything your mother is not
everything your mother points out
everything you think is wrong with you.

You fear these bits of him,
that baptized themselves to your frame
like the mismatched surnames
on your birth certificate
one for him, one for your mother.

Sometimes she catches you staring at her
but how can you tell her
you're searching for yourself,
and wishing she were a shade darker
to match your tone, or perhaps you were light
to an extent she understood to be beautiful?

Every image of yourself in mirrors
transmogrifies into
the infinite faces of the man
who never claimed you as his, or if he did,
he whispered it to a wind that died
before it found your ear.

You obsess about ways to exorcise
him from your body.
You wonder if you would love
this stripped version of you,
finally, untainted.

## Was it Manhood?

that famed thing,
that permitted him to palm his ears
to drown out my mother's screams
as I writhed out of her body
was it that venerated thing
that spurred his heels down the corridor
and out the swinging glass doors
    [] []
past the mango tree,
past the green city council rubbish bin
past the little boys kicking up dust in the football pitch
past the old man crouched, weeding maize in the roadside garden
    [past and past]
me growing my first tooth
me taking my first step
me saying 'Mama',
and all the words that came after,
words that were never
    [Dada]
past me at school stuttering:
*My-name-does-not-match-my-language-because*
    [],
my voice a thick tear rushing:
*I speak my mother's language because*
    []
past me skirting the shadow of my two surnames
through moons and years and places,
past my eyes trained over heads as I trace the black mole
on my mother's upper lip, in my mind
as they mouth, *'What about your father.'*
    []

## The Authentic

I was not to add water to the ghee
for the sauce to dunk the millet bread in
I was not to relegate the royal dish
to the tripe slurped by wretched peasants.

Had I forgotten you were descended of Chwezi,
elegant gods with moons for eyes,
bijou heads poised upon ringed necks
that stretched and stretched for days and days
over green hills that looped and looped
over their transcendental herd
of long-horned cattle?

You said your taste buds were whetted
by the bona fide sauce; ghee rhythmically beaten
with soft jelly tricep, to liquid song
of the hallowed egret, to mystical toppings
of white cow's soul. But peasant that I am,
all that reverence would be lost on me.

You hoped my flared nose would die with me
and your children would have your tapering one
that their tongues would be as light as the breeze
able to lilt silent 't's in syllables with ease
unencumbered by the weight of my thick tongue,
peasant that I am, how could I think I could be allowed
to poison the length of your sacred line?

## In His Absence

My paternal aunt names me for wealth
for herds wider than the reach of the sky
she names me for beauty
or how else will I bring cows home,
if the winds are not sooth-sayed
if in their ears my ageless beauty is not intoned,
with what will I catch a rich husband
if not with a smooth smooth skin
and hips the size of prize pumpkins
how will I be bestowed a name
and keep it girdled around my waist
to keep my man's eyes from falling
on others more bountiful than I?
She names me on her brother's behalf
even as his absence suffuses the birthing room
like a fog when the devil is awakening,
she still names me. She names me
so the clan will know it is I when the time comes,
for her brother to don his fatherhood cloak,
for him to receive the cows and ascend his throne
of a rocking chair, and see-saw as father of the bride.

*FREYA BANTIFF*

Freya Bantiff's writing achievements include the National Poetry Competition, Bridport Poetry Prize, Canterbury Poet of the Year, Bedford Poetry Competition, Walter Swan Poetry Prize, Timothy Corsellis Poetry Prize, Winchester Poetry Prize, Aesthetica Creative Writing Award, Mslexia Flash-Fiction Competition and Foyle Young Poet of the Year.

freyasophie394@btinternet.com

## The Photographer's Girlfriend

He is not interested in the rich pendants of sweat hanging
from the glassmaker's brow – only the heat of the day
which is blown, becoming an object, glossy

and desirable. This, amongst many things, is new to me.
It seems Venice has a market, stinking ammonia like a dying
sea. It appears he would choose a restaurant frontage

over a cat. *It's more precious,* he declares, *to take
a photo in analogue,* so when he shifts his camera away
from ordered capstones, archways, canals and onto me, I try

to feel flattered. Does it matter if I am just another
beautiful place that he is visiting? My spine, a stone
bridge bending backwards to his touch. My height, a balcony

for him to peer at himself. As for my eyes, I've seen
the distance he keeps from windows to frame and snap
the perfect shot. I can't feel the lens he points

at my retreating figure but recognise the sound of his shutter
behind me – as if I am hearing fireworks
without being able to see them.

*Suitcase in Tha Mai Ruak*


When I've packed a postcard of a langur
and a gibbon t-shirt, I get greedy, go for the twang

of a new friend's laugh that might stretch like
the web of a golden orb weaver so it vibrates

several continents away. Hills are more
difficult. They will not roll up – keep spilling

their pocketed lizards, lithe vines of snakes until
I follow them out under the trees where there are

twin butterfly wings in the mud. Yellow gilt
earrings dropped at midday. A stranger spots me.

Says it is the ants – they eat the fleshy bits as if
eating a rambutan. Consume the body of it.

The inner sweetness. *But look,* he says, *you see,*
*they must leave the most beautiful parts behind.*

# Side Order

You'll hate him later, as you overcook the details,
remembering his chip shop smile, his dead fish gaze,

the blood, the marinara streaking his white apron.
That, and the way his fingers gripped the towel,

the sizzling tray, like sausages escaped from the oven
as he filleted you with a look, backing you into

the alcove, pasta spitting between his hands.
That, and how your cannelloni pencil skirt constricted

around your calves, how his breath hit your face
with the smack of heat, how much his carcass

weighed as it pressed against your own. How you
stayed still, didn't thrash, floated up, out, away.

That, and the roll of his head, like a dice, deciding –
the tannoy switch, just out of reach – the screams

you suffocated as they pounded fists, hitting
boiling point in your chest. *What you gonna do about it?*

Later, you'll replay those words, scrub yourself
lobster red and still feel greasy. See him

slicing his face in two with a derisive laugh,
walking into the flame-glare restaurant

where the disco ball swivels like a giant eye
that blinked shut long ago and cannot bring itself to look.

*ALICE BRIDGWOOD*

Alice Bridgwood is a poet and ex-philosopher from Manchester. She works as a content producer, editor, and German translator. Alice tweets occasionally at @alicebridgwood

alice.bridgwood@gmail.com

## Dogsitting

*For Bao*


Been scrolling a lot, Reddit mostly – Am I the Asshole, Girl
Survival Guide. Screen time? Don't even want to know. Low
moors from the train window – what is this, a bloody
Brontë novel – vacant woman opposite counting scraps
of rubbish, nearly-missed stop, strange bed. Up at 6 am,
grumble out the door, check weather (mild) and Tinder (Paul),
past catcalling binmen and bankers, up onto the ancient
heath, this raw light new to me, this layered clay,
these heather-bruised heights – and you, leaping
in the faded grasses. I call your name and you come to me.

## Quaker meeting

Last week God had plenty to say:
        John was worried about his neighbours, you hear
the girls screaming but never an adult voice. A bloke on Facebook
   Marketplace
called Tash *that word* because she already gave away the mirror. Noah was
   plagued
by vaguely sexual fantasies of being a locust gorging on rich landscapes.
   Laura fucking
hates Coleridge, ok? Yusuf had been thinking about Psalm 108 (excuse
   me, Moab is my
*what now*?) But today only the dust motes are rising, they come and go
   with the traffic,
whirling up in the lulls between Amazon delivery trucks blocking the
   window, the circle
of bowed heads cleaved by the shaft of shifting light, then united by
   shadow
in the barren function room, its windows stained only by truck splash.
   Suddenly the silence
tautens, as if speaking would divide the void, send trees shooting up
   between the plastic chairs,
new buds bursting through the greige carpet, winged fowl wheeling under
   the strip lights –
because someone is standing, someone is moved to speak:
        with surprise, I realise it's me.

## Before missing a train in Kyoto

They say it's the last of the weather, but today
you can see the mountains, the herons strutting
     on the dam's cusp
         At the old station
where the river widens,
I will board the train that winds
       up to the cool groves
         with their many streams
I will take off my shoes and walk between the pines

Where the river widens, there it splits
parted by the rushes -
        they have the wind in them
On the far side, men are digging up the bank,
the necks of cranes cross
       against the white sky,
their wheels are hidden
       by the last of the grass

Where the river splits
       I will go down into the station
       I will go up into the mountains
       and be amongst them
I will take off my clothes and bathe in the hot spring

years praying to feel something, googling
am i doomed, saving up for silicone,
descending into that basement ann summers
in stoke-on-trent *thank you just browsing*,
rampant failures lined up in the bottom drawer,
rotating failures, rippled failures, 'realistic' failures,
pulsing thrusting bright pink failures. hot cute bunny when, why
bunny like warren-bound, bred for meat, born blind

*I've always liked shitting, it's the only time you really have a room of your*
*own, I remember the balmy airing cupboards of childhood, sticking my head*
*in as a treat, piles of damp Enid Blytons, the garden all Monet-ed by the*
*frosted glass, blood smear of wheelbarrow by the empty hutch*

the first time, the pulsing, rippling answer
to all that googling, pleasure leaping
from the thicket of years like a hare:
sinewed, solitary, seeing

Jessa Brown is from London. Her writing has been commended by Bloodaxe and she has been an *Acumen* Young Poet. She likes thinking about bodies and places – writing helps. Her work has been published in *The Mays* anthology, the *Young Writers' Anthology*, *Ink Sweat & Tears* and the *Brixton Review of Books*. Some of her poems were recently bought by the Design Council for the 2023 *Design for the Planet* Festival.

jessminniebrown@gmail.com

# Billie

Billie eating her breakfast in the dining hall with purpose. With a
purpose.
Billie laughing on your bedframe. Using Billie's name, using *Bil*. Using
her.
Billie in the club, soft body, soft dress, soft darkness; screaming country,
only she knows the words, the strobes strike her face with gouache,
her boots scuff the floor like cleft hooves.

Billie flirting, Billie hating you for flirting. Billie kissing,
her face eclipsed across the slow-mo, rainbowed room,
her hand still sticky from crying after losing her ID.
Billie finding the lecture theatre, Billie writing her thoughts,
lowering biscuits into tea like eggs into salted water,
breaking mugs, getting piercings, Billie who did not always know
what was fragile. Who was,

in summer, sunburnt, something
wrong, very wrong and not sure what.
Billie changing her clothes and surprised that you won't.
Billie going to Germany and going to France,
presumably tanning. She comes to your room,
her limp hair drying, and she's gotten thin!
Why has Billie gotten thin?

Billie face-down on the flat floor,
or bow-legged on the inch-thin ice,
her smile screwed. Billie not drinking,
Billie drinking too much at a self-satisfied
student poetry reading. Billie reading,
stringing herself out to fit in the crook
of a book she has to do

to get her degree. Billie getting her degree
and her parents, warily getting it with her.
Billie with her game face, telly face, trousers on,
moving house, Billie swamped with the pastoral joys

of a colander, a duvet in her milkmaid's arms.

Billie making chilli,
making you eat it,
mopping your tears up like blood,
amassing your months with a moon cup,
touching your spine where it hurts.
Billie bringing herself about,
going away, going to Ireland,
really gone. Billie in love,

the sound of Billie loving in the next room,
the sound of the tap's *tips* in this room, a sense
of the eggs in the pan, the sheets on the bed,
the log she put down beforehand burning for all to see.

Billie bringing you brownies, laying rat poison,
getting her banjo down off the wall. Billie
in bed without you, knotted, nervous; Billie smiling,
telling you how to fold your jumpers,
Billie in this part of Brockwell Park, really here
on the pressed grass from which you watched
two girls spring up, last minute.

However | swings, | is a riddle, and there is something of wonderland about |, something twee in the ins and outs of |. Obviously, there is the eye about the keyhole, the nose about the lock, the letterbox mouths off every now and then – but not in the voice of |. | is a wilful wall, perhaps, lapping at frame like wave on quay, but also a coffin, maybe, holding bodies and trappings briefly between states, behind bleached oak strains, the acned ghosts of locks long prised away, and hinges long creaked wide. The chain on | hangs like a wristwatch, limp by day, its loose jangles with the four un-working bells little mews to fathom: still, not quite the voice of |. | has never seen the counterpart of | – which is the other side, numbered and outwards facing. People leave and | cannot be opened, held to an enclave by shocks of steel and brass. Once back, | yawns a lack, falling away from foundations.

Isabelle Crow is a poet from Kent, who likes to write the sort of things that she would want to read. Currently, she is completing the MA in Poetry at UEA. Izzy enjoys posting on @isabellecrowwriting, an Instagram account that even her elderly grandparents are fans of.

izzygcrow@gmail.com

## Brother

I can't wait for when you're eighteen and I get to post the collage of pictures I've been collecting since you were six. Every time you were ours, but not entirely, but not that it ever mattered. We're going to smile as we bask in the light of our sunshine boy. The glow of a bonus brother. I can't wait for everyone to see your cheesy grin, and for them to see your little pop belly in that picture of you in the summer of 2019, when you were about to attempt your very first dive, posture of Tom Daley, and the tummy of third trimester. We were all so proud of you. It doesn't matter that you jumped face first. Real triers don't get it right first time. Dad is going to laugh at those pictures of you holding a beer, now that you can have a real one, and we're all going to pretend that you weren't tiny and huddled around the Christmas table with the adults, sipping on Bucks Fizz alongside the rest of us whilst you looked at us with shiny eyes and pretended to be tipsy. But that's between us. I'm going to project every first day of school picture on the side of our home. Year by year we're going to trace the way you changed. When all your teeth fell out before your tenth birthday, and when there were no more bald spots when you turned seven. Every picture is going to make us smile, especially the ones where you begin to tower over the rest of us, and Oliver is going to joke that he should've gone on tippy toes, because now he looks like the younger one. You're going to look at Mum with her watery eyes, proud that you have images to look back on, when before, there weren't any. There was no shortage of cameras, not in the place where we grew you. Our curly boy, I can't wait for all the memories we are yet to make, and all the dreams we're wishing for. I can't wait for you to point out the fractions of your childhood we shared, and for you to realise that an absence of six years doesn't mean you aren't whole. It always should've been you.

## Pinkification

we're not kids anymore,
two little girls who used to
plait their hair together
in the playground.
strands of blonde and brunette,
interwoven and undeveloped.

i still look through our pictures,
the photobooth we went in
the year i started my period,
when we grabbed onto each other
under the cold blue flash of light,
giggling into the screen that was frosted
with fingerprints.

i make a wish
on an eyelash, that we can be
those girls again, with tongues
tinted pink from sour sweets,
listening to pop princess
as we stuck together a collage
of pictures of how we wanted our life to be,
a life we were convinced we would live.
tiny images we had printed off or cut out
of magazines into neat bubbles.

i'm always going to miss you,
like how an adult misses her teddy.
the one with the matts in the fur from
being too well loved.
from being held too much.
i should've told you a little more,
how lucky i was to have you, to need you.
we should never have forgot the words
to the only song we could sing.

you were my good luck text before a big exam,
but we've graduated now.

## Breakup Poem

he loved her like a whisper,
so sometimes all she heard was silence.

she loved him in the chapped lips
on a cold day sort of way,
when you try to lick the cracks of skin away.
tugging at them with your teeth.
tongue as a fleshy eraser.

she loved him at high speed,
a flimsy bit of metal rattling down
the motorway, hands gripping
at the steering wheel.
she was thelma and she was louise.

she loved him like a budget wine,
when she would swill him in her glass,
flushed cheeks watching the liquid dance,
going red and raw
when all she smelt was vinegar.

she loved him like a footprint,
the one she carved in the grass,
on the foggy walk home,
as the air was holding her hand
and promising to tuck her into bed.

she loved him when they shouted,
because at least it meant he listened.

## Mean Something

Why do we always remember the plane journey there,
but never the one home,
when our tan's a bit brighter and we get a few extra freckles,
messaging in the group chat about how
*I think I'm getting my sparkle back.*

It must mean something,
like when the girl sitting next to you in class
has a sticky note of calories stuck to the case of her phone.
*Apple. 95. KitKat. 104.*
Etched in neat lines, the guidelines of her mind.

It must mean something,
the way I can't help but love without control,
drawing pictures in my dreams,
of every life I want to live,
whilst pencilling you into every frame.

It must mean something,
when my little brother has to pull his hoodie down,
just because I don't have hair like his,
an afro that we celebrate with braids and twists,
skin that is showered with cocoa butter kisses.

It must mean something,
the way my dog tip taps on the bathroom door,
when I'm cheeks pressed against cold tiles,
scratching, scratching to be let in,
until I'm ready to put myself down again.

Rupert Dorey lives in Hastings where he works as a mental health nurse. Originally trained as a fine artist, he has been writing for over twenty years. He is currently preparing his first poetry collection having previously only shared his writing between close friends.

rupertdorey1@gmail.com

## High Falls

Whitewater down black rock
    sometimes
    I'm so sure of something

    and find I'm
    completely wrong.

And though I said I had a feeling
    of the shape of things to come

    and still think in a way
    that I do

    don't know how deep
    the water is
    in this swimming hole

    I just
    don't know.

Told you I don't think
    you're being late this month
    means

    what we talked about

    that we'll go back to England
    with only
    tanned arms

    and the money we saved
    from the truck.

But I don't know if I were wrong—

> would I want it
> that way.

Found the wheel of an old log floating
> low in the water

> put my arms around it
> the bark to my bare chest

> and kicking my legs
> I swam us around.

You and Liv sat on the bank
> underneath the trees

> I can't hear you but I know
> what you're
> talking about.

And I'm starting to feel more
> and more in these days

> whatever happens I'll meet it
> halfway.

I sit out on the rock
> in full sun

> whitewater coming
> down.

## Harry Howard Avenue

All this coffee and
    blackbeans
    coffee can and eggs

        eggs fried in an iron pan
        tipbeans hissing wet.

I'm sat out on the back porch
    this morning
    under peeling paintwork
    wasps

        sound o' cars
        from the road.

Bright top o' that cloud
    above the garage roof

        black and white cat
        sat out on the lawn

        black cat's nowhere
        to be seen.

And haven't seen anyone all morning
    don't expect to
    all afternoon.

MEXICO, IRENE SANCHEZ
    PEACH PIE COFFEE

        behind me the wind moves the back door
        on its hinges saying
        *heeey.*

There's nearly eight hundred dollars upstairs under the bed
        in the room we're staying in

        and look at that red plastic watering can
        on the porch half in the sun

        I'll never do a day's work again.

Though tomorrow
        I'm down on the rota

        Eliya's coming by
        at ten.

And God has every tree for an arm
        and my waving toes
        for a heart

        getting the back legs o' this chair
        in the right place

        my weight holds me
        'gainst the wall.

Black beans and eggs
        in swimming shorts
        reading back pages alone

        the stories of Xiao Hong,
        Berlin's *Home Again*

And if I don't write anything meaningful
        well
        did I tell anybody I would—

        when this evening's still
        just an idea

        one that I like.

Coming out onto the back porch
    pick up my biro again.

A week or two
    o' mornings like this

    I'll have filled this
    book.

E. M. Fawkes is a writer based in coastal Suffolk, having unearthed her poetic voice during the final year of her BA at UEA. Forever collecting written fragments of the world around her, she seeks to excavate and illuminate the extraordinary everyday through her poetry, and particularly, to make language new again.

emfawkes80@gmail.com

## Hurting Gymnastics

eyeroll wetly in skull
I'm all-a-rosacea
finding the berries of my first time

it's hurting fantastic        like salt on new skin
it's hurting fantastic        kidnapped kidgloves
it's hurting cataclysmic     a fragrant herb penalty

I got everything out
& you monthed me
till I became the moon you watched nights by

a hurting gymnastics

now your mouth
hurls lilies into emptiness

package of thanks

I sit here eating
the light I was meant
to be cleaning

& regret nothing.

## Illuminary

white with globes

thread of light & the Ms we used to make birds with

so much green for the night

two waves unstart themselves

your back is hurting beautiful

licked black gating gathering itself into posts & poles

pine-gold starwork stiffened into something nightly

pearls in bed of tongue

barely one blue from the next

splash of light down steps

wet & orbular

& we are polar sometimes

roof a stretch of oesophagus

thumbtack three threes on that line between sea & sky

always telescoping &

now I turn on

all the coloured lights

over my bed &

think of you

## Chandelier Silence

You sitting there, copying light like a coast,
washing me something morning-aged,
only a cupful, & grinning like a swan.

I came like a childcall into fog,
pulled my sickness up by the belthooks,
made the underpurple my light to read by,

renewed the last dead arch of my throat,
drank back the angelshare, covered vertebrae
with water, a whole skyworks on our spines,

pinned my hair with bristling sprigs, their white
hot corners dripping in & out of us, outgrew
each syrinx, ingrew each bough heaving

with the weight of the new year, let clouds fowl
dark as cigarsmoke between us, claimed
cartography my climbed tree, listened

to moonleaks by the quick black
flick of windowed sky & rewrote us
in years of newspaper. You started

naming all the red songs you know,
but not the one you needed, 'cause
revenge is a spectrum. Revenge

is this restless language
roiling through
chandelier silence,

rotating sunstoned,
heavy with little Sri
Lankas. Language my

last violence. I could sleep

on the velveteen bottoms
of caskets for days after,

funfaired with quiet.

Kana Hozoji is a poet who writes both in Japanese and English, and often bilingually. Having studied creative writing poetry and Japanese culture and literature, her poems questions conventions of language and explores nonlinguistic aspects of them. Her poems have appeared in *Incollepoetry* and *Sink Review*.

kanah1021@gmail.com

Words have meanings but sounds have meanings too, individual sounds, sounds that are separate from each other but never completely separate or never completely intact, when the sound begins it never ends it is just ringing in someone else's room you cannot enter


CU-CU-M-BA
she pronounced it like this
the vegetable she held it in her hand the
way you hold a weapon
but when she held it,
it was a torch

CU-CU-M-BA
she said and laughed with her throat and teeth,
you love her
for that

CU-CU-M-BA
did not embody
the green fragile vegetable you
picture a torch in her hand
this vegetable you have never eaten warm but the
vegetable and the flames they are
complimentary colors aren't they,
yes
you agree that it was on fire

you offer a vegetable from your language
JA-GA-I-MO
she mouths the word as you push it through
JA-GA-I-MO
what comes out is warmer, shapes of heated coal
when she spoke
the vegetable was
cooked, you
take turns tossing it

around, warming up the kitchen
danced with lit torches in hands and breathed
steam, spitting
dust that covered them,
dust
rolling
off bodies, she laughed
with her throat and teeth and you laughed with your nose
it was a
matsuri
of some
sort

## Moons, you fit them in your eyes

the moon was the size of an eye so you replace it you blow on it softly and it begins to multiply two four eight sixteen multiply so quickly you are not bothered to pick up the ones that roll around your feet multiply so quickly it was the moon not the star but it glows and while you look for the source of the blinding bright you can no longer see you realize this a little later than your eyes lose sight the multiplying moons on your palms feel enough your palms are overstimulated nothing more is required

multiplying stops

the final moon rolls out of your palm you
crouch down careful not to sit on them waft your hands until you pick one up replace one, two, you, slowly placing them in your socket go look for something

TANUVI JOE

Tanuvi is an Indian poet and climate journalist based in Norwich. She is presently pursuing her MA in Poetry at UEA.

tanuvijoe9@gmail.com
rufflingwings.tech

## Poets and Poetry

*I*
*But*

it's bogus.
What you don't say about the trees
in Earlham Park
and how they are forced
to meet your disposable
coffee cups, plastic hiding
in sight, rotting the roots beneath
the grass your shoes get wet from.

Poetry workshop turns quickly
into a manmade disaster
where these cups multiply
like the biblical loaves of bread
one to feed
one to disappear the feed.

Mary Oliver dedicated her life to trees
so we could ask questions.
Alas, we read her poems next to those cups
her ghost catching us
by our breath and tying it
in with the lining where
one day, they will manifest as hospital tubes
our lungs, then, toxified roots.

Please keep breathing all that lining.

*II*
*It is bogus.*


What you don't say about the sun
in Earlham Park
and how the coke
spills from your mouth while Bernadette Mayer
is recited, pushing
the sun further into nonexistence.

Poetry workshop quickly turns
into a manmade disaster
gobbling up poems, puking
out the world's no. 1 plastic polluter
alongside paper plastic cups.
This is not a safe
space for me and neither
it should be for you.

Jorie Graham poeticises
extinction and human impact on earth
so we could have an empty bin.
Alas, we read her poem next to the extinction
campaigners, her pencil giving
up while she drafts her new piece.

Meanwhile, the worms swear to abandon our bodies,
making way for the landfills as they do want to meet their creators.

*III*
*This*


is bogus.
Who am I
to tell you what isn't said
about the trees and the sun at Earlham Park?
For it is I
who loses sense
of extinction when the next meal
is to be decided.

Poetry workshop was a manmade disaster
As I realised how my first poem
about the climate crisis made everyone
in the room, no one in the poem.

Does anyone write poems about how the sun and the trees at Earlham
Park are being driven into extinction by the paper plastic cups and coke
at Earlham Hall and the meat purchases at Tesco on Bluebell road?

Do I?
Do you?
Or have we turned away from this world?

It is the turn of the sun and the trees
But they say                    soon                    it will be our turn.

Lauren Sheerman is a poet, teacher and arts producer living in Norwich. She was Artist in Residence at The Pod Coventry in 2018 and 2019 and has had work published in *14 magazine* and *Earthlings zine*.

laurenjanesheerman@gmail.com
www.laurensheerman.co.uk

## sometimes i sit in my car

wearing my favourite shirt like i'm real
i pretend to be bored in traffic & ok i'll sing along
& roll my eyes & pretend to be rushing & yes
i'll stand in a queue at the supermarket with my arms crossed
a basket of bougie food at my feet & i'll hold my keys like i own
something
& sometimes i even get home from a short trip to buy something i've
forgotten
i might linger in my car like i have a whole family waiting for me inside
like i have so much responsibility for a happiness i don't even know
for a life i don't even want & how could i it's like craving those plastic
high heels from the nineties & there's that smell to everything
like sweetly perfumed plastic on the barbie body & everything
i'd slung out of the window & i'm home & i refresh my emails
i open the messages on my phone & i open my diary at today
like i have so much to do
today i have so much
but it's a lie i sit on my bed
in my pants like another day worn.

## everything must go and let it

how each thing each memory each person spreads
like thick butter across my diaphragm like a yard sale
and yes this is a sticky thing this is a greasy thing
O this is a coffee thing but I cannot sell it
because it was my father's and it is a priceless precious old thing
and anyway I cannot account for it for selling coffee pots
for missing a person because of my sentimentality
and because I haven't done my taxes because I was busy
at the yard sale and I was in my yard for three whole days
because no one wanted to buy my greasy wares
and it rained the whole time and not a thing sold nothing cleaned
even the rain is dirty now and all my things
are thrown across the muscled lawn that helps me breathe
each thing each memory each person piled up panting like a puppy

## holy well ritual

holy well is two pools with tree
reflections pushed around by rain
drops like impressionist paint
branches gesture offerings
little arms of moss wave to the surface
pennies leaves cigarette butts open the veil
of the water with a stroke and the church
glares over the wall —

down five steps into the small pool you
break open the water like an egg
ask yourself how you want to arrange
your day and say it aloud to the corn
kernels which float as the sun drops
into the day drop into the yolk of yourself
leaf enters air enters water enters skin
under is the place to enter say aloud
this is god cold and she is water —

Harriet Truscott is a poet, editor and arts organiser. She's part of a collaborative Book Arts group and has co-organised two successful literary festivals. Her poetry has been published in a number of literary journals in both the UK and the US, including *Oxford Poetry*, *Magma* and *Atlanta Review*.

harriet.truscott@gmail.com
www.hmtruscott.co.uk

# Heir of all the writers and the rest

Vladimir Putin is the poet of our time!

Metaphor is now the law. The special warry operation
is merely in the service of the special wordy operation.

Leave a page blank, and you'll be beaten
in case it's filled out later with plain speaking.

The opprosition is locked up and so they should be,
for Putin is the great Vortifuturedadaist, the one
who shoots sound willy-shally at the world.

If Putin wishes wrench and birthday to rhyme, they do,
and now words have as many syllalalables as he decreereereereerees
for lines to march with forceful feet.

BOOOOM!
Applause for the poem, everyone!

Truly Putin is the worthy heir
of – what were their names again,
those great poets of the past?

## Warning – do not overload

I am the TipTop washing machine
repair man. I step close
to the washing machine
and smile.

*TipTop,* I say, and the white box
shudders backwards. I lay
a calming hand upon it.
*TipTop*, I say, diagnosing
its quivering reluctance
to make things fresh.

*TipTop*, I say, more forcefully,
laying a hand upon its door,
pulling out its soap tray, slipping a foot
beneath its silver belly. With a lurch,
it flees, out of the kitchen,
out the back door, squeezes by the wheelie bins –
but I am ready for it. I've seen
all this before. I know the way
a washing machine is overwhelmed
by shivering fear of the requirement
to undo each day's stains, the claim
to make us new, begin us again
at our beginnings.

I am the washing machine repair man. I
come at each washing machine with confidence.
*TipTop*, I say, and it, weeping,
opens its glass mouth.

## Sex with a man with a JCB

I said
you're the first man I've shagged who's got a JCB.
He said
that you know of.
I said                                                        yes

I said
I think men tend to tell you if they've got a JCB.
He said
you mean we like to brag about our equipment.
I said                                                        yes

He said
you think digging's about the depth, the plunge –
mechanical, repetitive, completely unskilled
but let me tell you –
I said                                                        yes

He said
it's reaching out a cupped hand, stroking the earth,
feeling the ground give way, sun-soaked above,
below damper and darker  –
                                                             yes

it's how the soil shines as the digger lip slides,
as you nibble and delve and lick at the silt;
lifting, tilting  –  letting it fall
and then how the earth cascades dark through the air.
I said                                                        yes
                                                             yes
                                                             yes
                                                             yes
                                                             yes

He said
I'm thinking about getting a second JCB
I said                                                        oh

Adrienne Wilkinson lives in Norwich, UK. Her debut pamphlet *repeating mouths* was published by Broken Sleep Books in 2021, and her work has appeared in magazines such as *bath magg, Ink Sweat & Tears*, and *The Manchester Review.* In 2021 she was shortlisted for the Bridport Poetry Prize.

Twitter: @adr_wilkinson

## Extract from 'SPECULUM'

o mouthed thing
donut theory of the universe
bigger on the inside
                        & insurmountable

body in waiting
something about black holes
huge                   & imminent


         &


if i could look in
would i see
river flowing backwards
viscus flowers blooming

mirror seeing
      myself backwards
cervix looking doctor right in the eye
me up here

# flowers

opening reminding me of ovulation yes i want to fuck the spring to be more like spring to become spring until dewy snowdrops unfurl from my stomach daffodils elbow themselves out of my ribcage honeysuckle from my neck yes i want to feel that life stir inside me & wake up stronger feeling the sun's warmth radiate out of me lavendula pooling inside me & my body is turning to dusk later & later so my skin is inky & goosebumped & in the morning birdsong limbers my joints & chest & stirrings underground bring the smell of vetiver from my pores something is building / spring is coming

## women walk through the woods collecting ferns

enjoying the mulch of earth / the dirt on their fingers / even a shoe slips off / revealing 18th century toes / unfurling from the pinch / touching the earth / the wet mud / letting feet sink in / spread / women alone / away from the city / skirts hitched up / grasping the fern / with their fingers / the scratch of a bramble / on thigh

showing off / for one another / thinking / how many times / with generous hands / to the earth / time running on / out / how long it takes to deplete something / how quickly it could happen / imagining husbands / and smog

lovingly / knowingly / bringing living things home / to arrange in clean containers / moments like that / touching them / not picking up pens / brushing off dirt / husbands / the conjugal bed / and that glass box / of fronds / decorating the corner

## it's a bit too cringe like

putting a cat on a diet
visiting the london eye
there's something not quite right about
eating prunes
or having a mechanical neck injury
from tension in your trapezius
nurturing your inner child
'doing the work' thinking
am i cringe but free?
going on instagram feels cringe anyway
is everything cringe but the moment?
sometimes even walking slow
or saying goodbye does it
being the only one who
  finishes your meal
having the signs of a lifetime
scored into your body
savouring the moment
stopping to touch the wet brick on a wall
or looking at a sunset

financial troubles are definitely cringe
being an only child thinking about what will happen
when your parents are old and dying
waiting for your partner to kiss you
there is so much potential for damage
before you've even left the bedroom
in the bedroom you've cringed the most
and thinking about yourself in the past is worse
governments are the cringiest thing
  thing with many eyes and legs
  hungry devouring thing
  moving itself towards you
 solemnity in
  a bad wig

Rebecca Zeman read English at Jesus College, Cambridge and worked as a journalist and copywriter before taking her MA. She lives with her husband and whippet in West Sussex, where – apart from writing – she likes to grow flowers, comb junk shops, pick up litter and wild swim.

rebecca.dowman@cantab.net

# A dude in disguise

Like Princess Fiona inside Shrek's ogress,
Hoffman's high heel-tottering Tootsie,
Superman beneath Clark Kent's specs,
you were always a dude in disguise.

Yesterday, the dude slipped out
leaving your capsule – worn, wrinkled, wan.
Pain stamped on your face,
her body blows bleaching your eyes.

Lining that chair like an orthotic in a shoe
you hadn't the power to stand,
let alone scale a conversation.
Your body, the tormentor,

mining the path to your landline,
hijacking speech with lung-gashing coughs,
that slight slope to your book club a black run
aborting reading, your one escape route.

Awake at 3am, I see your face, pale as an endsheet.

In the light, I draw on illustrated pages.
You crying in a café over my coach-crash romance,
us, gig-goers, chanting *I would walk five hundred miles*,
you on a chair, hanging curtains you made for my first flat.

Your pilot light sparked, you pull out
the East End trans woman holding court
in that East Berlin bookshop, my wedding,
our picnic by the Glyndebourne ha-ha,

then, like the removal boxes aren't stacked on your coffin,
you say your daughter's family will live here.
I squeak 'Not for some time,'
kiss your springy badger hair, say 'I love you.'

I only get the 'You too'
but as I look back at your window, dude,
you're upright, waving with both hands
like an aircraft marshaller with paddles.

## A Healthy Omen

Like Penelope clinching comeback king Ulysses,
Arundel opened its empty arms and squeezed.

The town crier raised her white-gloved hand
and clanged the *Oyez!* with her brass school bell,

the mayor garlanded our local heroes
liberators from years of privation hell,

the MP rolled out to snip the ribbon
blue, like his shirt, tie and disposition:

like that all-at-sea son of Ithaca
a town chemist had been a long time coming.

O Asclepius!, son of Apollo, great God of Medicine,
you heard us! You read our petitions – after a fashion,

OK, this sanctum may not dispense NHS prescriptions
but among fudge, junk and art shops beyond description,

a well of plasters, perfume and painkillers
cannot but quicken our dicky hearts and thrill us.

We enter the stone gates, making sacrifice within
acquiring unwanted unguents and cures for wind,

as old ladies tantalise the chemist delegation
with tales of friends in macular degeneration,

as if to say, 'Rest easy – you've set down
your anchor in an epic plague town.'

On being asked to round up my charity shop purchase price
to £10 to help children with cancer this Christmas

'Your bum looks as big as Belgium in that and no I didn't sleep well
as your spare bed has more ruts than a rural track and I would rather
chomp my right arm off than have another helping and I can't be arsed
to look round your garden and does he really think I can't tell he's still
drinking? and I would prefer slugs savaging my seedlings to seeing
your holiday snaps and I will NOT sponsor your daughter in her school
silenceathon and I don't care how little meat you say you eat, you're still
raping the planet and slaughtering sentient beings and no my whippet
is not a rescue – she is the heiress of champions.'

'Yes, of course.'

## Cutting down sunflowers

Wide-ankled women in poppy-speared hats
zimmer in waves from colonies of retirement flats
cutting up old boys bristling with brass.
Scouts with pennants muster by the bridge,
a woman tells a child she can't have a medal –
'You earn them, darling, like swimming badges.'
Cafés arm sun-swollen ranks with pagers
to sound the alert when they can claim their coffees:
it's Remembrance Sunday and Arundel expects.

The town crier disciplines her tri-cornered hat,
as worthies and choristers slow step
past antique shops to the memorial square.
The church bells give way. We suffer
the little children's bloody war poems,
the mayor confirms age shall not weary them,
the vicar, gabbling to get in before 11, calls –
against all odds – for peace. A cannon cracks
somewhere in the castle grounds. A baby bellows,
people covertly stroke their dogs. I pray
my coffee bleeper won't sabotage The Silence.
Straighter than the half-dressed flagpole,
a man clenches his hat like the neck of the Hun.

The cannon's 'at ease' stirs flagpole man,
who replaces his creased hat as the heirs
of those First War cheerleaders lay
haemorrhage-red wreaths.
Again in rank order the Duke leads the charge
                    next in line, the young earl
                              his countess
                                        the Rotary Club and Lions.
Our innocents – the infants' school – come last.

After walking home with neighbours,
dressed in job interview smarts,
I cut down the sunflowers
I raised from seed
that stood tall against the fence
semaphoring hope all summer.
They had their time.

## Wherever you are, Dad, I hope it's hot

My sister is whirling like a culinary deity, moving so fast it's hard to tell whether she has six arms or four. Drinks? Checking turkey, drinks? Checking potatoes, 'no, I'm fine, Mum', checking greens, drinks? Checking pudding, drinks? 'Don't worry, Dad. Dan, please swab that up.' Checking. Her first year married and we're still Christmas present. Posing as a normal family for her new husband, my elder brother absent, a festive physical fight is less likely than usual. A Christmas miracle: everything comes together. We sit down. Pressed napkins straighten. Plates of Delia Smith veer by. Goblets blow bubbles. Dad chucks a hand grenade: 'This food's not hot.'

Meltdown.

Tracy snatches the plates. We move away from the table. The TV reignites. Dad reclines on the sofa. The oven whirrs. I wince with my sister's pain. I try to hug her. She pushes me away, again. Thirty minutes later, we crawl back in the crater. When my appetite returns, I invite my parents to a Cambridge superhall: a three-course meal at long mahogany tables in a medieval hall with mandatory black gowns and braying white men throwing food overlooked by dons at top table and Henry VIII. Proud Parent Paradise. Latin grace may have been too long, the hot plates too cool. The meal arrives, Dad pulls out the pin. I scream. 'It's not about the food, muppet. Do I really have to get some frazzled waiter to blast your meal, as the entire college observes you – ergo me – are Beyond Bonkers?' He confirms that I do.

The microwave pings. I reclaim my reheated bowl of half-eaten porridge. The golden syrup and oats are erupting in molten streams. Breakfast Etna.

*ACKNOWLEDGEMENTS*

This anthology brings together poetry written by the 2022–23 students of UEA's MA in Creative Writing: Poetry.

We are hugely grateful for the support of Philip Langeskov and the UEA School of Literature, Drama and Creative Writing in partnership with Egg Box Publishing, without whom this anthology would not have been possible.

Our poetry tutors were Tiffany Atkinson, Holly Corfield-Carr, Jeremy Noel-Tod and Sophie Robinson. During a difficult year, you continued to teach with dedication and skill, helping us each to develop our writing along our own paths. We deeply appreciate all of the insights you offered.

We would like to thank the many other tutors and UEA staff who contributed to our studies. From performing poetry on park benches to pitching an anthology to a publisher, we've been encouraged to challenge ourselves in ways that we never expected. Too many to name individually, you include the outstanding tutors of the School of Literature, Drama and Creative Writing, the ever-welcoming archivists, and those who sold us coffee when we were in desperate need. The LDC Poetry PhD students offered support and critiques from our first day, while the team at Dragon Hall ran an inspirational literary events programme from our first evening.

Many of the UEA MA poets in this anthology were supported by scholarships, and we would like to thank the donors, together with all those friends and family who supported us in other ways.

And finally, here's to all our fellow students. Without each others' thoughtful readings, generous praise, and steady encouragement, the poetry in this anthology could not have been written. Thank you!

Lillian Akampurira Aujo and Harriet Truscott

UEA MA Creative Writing Anthologies: Poetry and Translated Literature

First published by Egg Box Publishing, 2023
Part of the UEA Publishing Project Ltd.

International © retained by individual authors

This book is sold subject to the condition that it shall not, by way of trade or otherwise, be lent, resold, hired out, stored in a retrieval system, or otherwise circulated without the publisher's prior consent in any form of binding or cover other than that in which it is published and without a similar condition including this condition being imposed on the subsequent purchaser.

A CIP record for this book is available from the British Library
Printed and bound in the UK by Imprint Digital

Designed by Emily Benton Book Design
emilybentonbookdesign.co.uk

Distributed by BookSource
50 Cambuslang Road
Cambuslang
Glasgow
G32 8NB
+44 (0)141 642 9192
booksource.net

ISBN 978-1-915812-23-0